THREE STORIES

Kurt Schwitters

WITH A TRIBUTE BY E. L. T. MESENS

EDITED BY JASIA REICHARDT

TATE PUBLISHING

This anthology first published in 2010 by order of the Tate Trustees by Tate Publishing, a division of Tate Enterprises Ltd, Millbank, London SW1P 4RG
www.tate.org.uk/publishing

British Library Cataloguing in Publication Data
A catalogue record for this book is available from the British Library
ISBN: 978 1 85437 909 2

Library of Congress Cataloging in Publication Data
Library of Congress Control Number 2010910052

Designed by Libanus Press
Reproduction by DL Interactive Ltd, London
Printed and bound by DZS Grafik, Slovenia
Front cover: Kurt Schwitters, *With a Slit*, c.1924–5, courtesy of Lord's Gallery, © DACS 2010

The versions of the three stories reproduced in this volume are taken from Kurt Schwitters, *Die literarischen Werk*, vol.3, *Prosa 1931–1948*, ed. Friedhelm Lach, Cologne 1975, reprinted 1998. The poem 'London Symphony' is reproduced from Kurt Schwitters, *Die literarischen Werk*, vol.1, *Lyrik*, ed. Friedhelm Lach, Cologne 1973, reprinted 1998. Some of the texts exist in several variants, as detailed below.

'The Flat and Round Painter'
The original was produced on a typewriter, complete with marginal illustrations and was entitled 'The Story of the Flat and Round Painter'. It is likely to have been drafted in 1941, when Schwitters was interned in a prisoner-of-war camp on the Isle of Man. It was translated by Heinz Beran. The original is held in the Themerson Archive in London. This publication does not take into account the hand-written amendments in the original typescript.

'The Idiot'
The original was produced on a typewriter and is held in the Themerson Archive in London. It reproduces a translation of the Norwegian original 'Den fattige i anden', jointly authored by Kurt and Ernst Schwitters. Kurt Schwitters later revised this first version of the translation (published in Kurt Schwitters, *Die literarischen Werk*, vol.3, *Prosa 1931–1948*, ed. Friedhelm Lach, Cologne 1975, reprinted 1998, pp. 325–6). The Norwegian as well as the revised English original typescript are to be found in the Sprengel Museum in Hanover – on loan from the Kurt and Ernst Schwitters Foundation. There's also another variant of the translation held there.

'The Landlady'
The original manuscript is a typed copy from the Themerson Archive in London, probably produced by Edith Thomas, which was later mistakenly dated 1941/42. The text here was produced in Ambleside in 1945.

'London Symphony'
Reprinted from Stefan Themerson, *Kurt Schwitters in England*, London 1958, p. 51. The original was probably the hand-written manuscript by Kurt Schwitters dated 1942, which today is to be found in the Tate Archive, London, on loan from a private collection. A second, hand-written version of *London Symphony*, dated 1946, by Friedhelm Lach, is in the Sprengel Museum, Hanover, on loan from the Kurt and Ernst Schwitters Foundation. There is also a typed version in the Themerson archive.

Dr Isabel Schulz, Executive Director, Kurt and Ernst Schwitters Foundation, Hanover

CONTENTS

LIFE IS A STORY

Schwitters was in his early fifties when he wrote these three stories. 'The Flat and Round Painter' was written in 1941 on the Isle of Man, where he was interned as an enemy alien. Translated by Heinz Beran, it was duplicated on foolscap paper with a couple of drawings. 'The Landlady' and 'The Idiot' were written in London, after his release later that year. As in any fairy tales, the reader is presented with the unexpected. But the oddness of these stories extends into realms of the absurd, even the subversive. The stories that Schwitters wrote throughout his career changed with time, like his circumstances and his art. And art, he said, is 'play with serious problems'.

At the mention of Kurt Schwitters, we don't immediately think of a poet or storyteller. He is famous as the master of collage, who in 1919 chose the name 'Merz' for his own brand of Dada, from the title Kommerz und Privat Bank. But of course, he was also prolifically creative as painter, typographer, sculptor, poet, writer of stories, and the maker of assembled environments – the three Merzbauten [Merz-buildings] made from found materials. The first of these was in Hanover, the next in Lysaker, Norway, and the last in Little Langdale in the Lake District, still unfinished when he died. His aim was to unify art and non-art. Merz, he said, was a 'total vision of the world'. Little wonder that Herbert Read called him 'a complete artist'.

Schwitters found himself in Britain in 1937 by chance. The political unrest in Germany prior to World War II precipitated his escape from his native Hanover to Norway (he had spent holidays there in the past). With the invasion of Norway in 1940, Schwitters and his son Ernst fled to Scotland. As German nationals, they were interned in the Hutchinson Square Camp on the Isle of Man. Released 17 months later, Schwitters came to live in London, first in St Stephen's Crescent in Bayswater, and then in Westmoreland Road in Barnes. Here, in 1941, he met Edith Thomas (whom he called 'Wantee'), and in the summer of 1945 they moved together to Ambleside, where he died in January 1948.

Schwitters' stories and poems, like his art, are autobiographical, all woven around his experiences. The bus tickets and wrappers that he glues into his collages belong to a time and a place, as do the words and letters he selects from printed ephemera. 'I like to compose my paintings from the leftovers of daily refuse',[1] he wrote, and his surroundings were all alive with raw material: advertisements, shop windows, discarded objects, fragments of wood or wire lying on the pavement, some of which he took home to use.

When he first met Stefan Themerson, he was fashioning a piece of wire that he'd found on a bombsite into a space-sculpture. They happened to be sitting next to each other, and Themerson was curious about what he was doing. This meeting took place at a PEN conference held to celebrate Milton's *Areopagitica* on 26 August 1944 at the French Institute. It was the beginning of a friendship that lasted until Schwitters' death. They had similar avant-garde tastes for experiment, not least their shared curiosity about language and the celebration of nonsense.

Schwitters visited Stefan and Franciszka Themerson in Maida Vale. He made some collages in Franciszka's studio and later sent his poems and stories to Stefan. Subsequently Stefan wrote two major texts about Schwitters. The first was given as a lecture in the Gaberbocchus Common Room on 25 February 1958, entitled 'Kurt Schwitters' Last Notebook'. This became the basis of Themerson's

1 Kurt Schwitters, 'CoEM', *Transition*, June 1936, p.91

book, *Kurt Schwitters in England*, published by Gaberbocchus Press later that year. The book included several of Schwitters' poems and stories. The second text – 'Kurt Schwitters on a Time Chart', which places Schwitters in a historical context and discusses some shared ideas – was published in *Typographica* 16, in December 1967. (The three stories included here did not appear in either of these publications.)

Publication of *Kurt Schwitters in England* coincided with the important Schwitters exhibition at the Lord's Gallery at 26 Wellington Road in St John's Wood, October–November 1958. To celebrate the occasion, 'A Tribute to Kurt Schwitters' by E.L.T. Mesens appeared in *Art News and Review* on 11 October 1958. Mesens, who knew Schwitters in the 1920s, had been an enthusiastic supporter of his work. His essay describes the efforts to create an appetite for Schwitters' oeuvre in face of the lack of interest and understanding that confronted him in England. In the following issue of *Art News and Review*, Ernst Schwitters responded with some corrections, to which Mesens replied. The two men saw Schwitters from different points of view.

Schwitters would not have been surprised his work and humour celebrated opposites. He said that Merz meant smiling on sad occasions and being serious at happier times. In the world of Merz, all rules were arbitrary.

Jasia Reichardt

THE FLAT AND ROUND PAINTER

Once upon a time there was a painter-chap who painted his paintings in the air – not plain flat figures with flat paint-brushes on flat canvas, which were painted so flat that they really looked flat and plain – but he painted round figures round in the air.

So he painted a queen. She had an enormous velvet skirt on her legs, and a crown on her head, and a shock of hair under the crown, which looked like a cake, so beautifully was it done. And her graceful arms with slim fingers and the big brilliant rings on her fingers moved, as the fingers of a queen used to move.

Then the wind came and blew Her Majesty the Queen away, and the painter observed this display with anxious eyes. The queen wobbled and bubbled in the air, and swayed and waved just as the air under her waved and swayed. Suddenly she grew quite thick round the middle, blew herself up, burst, and fell in two pieces. The skirt with the legs by itself, and the bosom with the crown by themselves. When the painter-chap saw this, he got very serious, and painted, in a great hurry, a page-boy in the air. Not a plain flat page-boy with flat paint-brush on flat canvas who was painted so flat he really looked flat and plain, but he painted a round page-boy round in the air. He had a tightly fitting dress on his thin legs, and big longing eyes under his page-crop, and his fingers were as thin as graceful matches.

Then the wind came and blew the page-boy in the direction of the queen who had burst. He trembled and scrambled in the air, and he shivered and schwittered, like the air under him schwittered and shivered. And his eyes and fingers were longing to put the queen in order again. Therefore, he kicked his little legs in the air so that he might get ahead a bit more quickly, and he slipped several times and fell, for it was cold, and the air was slippery with ice.

Suddenly as he reached the parted parts of the departing queen, he grew quite thick round the middle, blew himself up, burst, and fell in two pieces.

The tightly fitting dress with the legs by itself, and the longing eyes with the fingers by themselves, for he was quite near his adored queen.

Now, his legs and his fingers had still kept the direction of the fast chase. And thus his legs put themselves under the fat bosom of the queen, and the longing eyes with the match fingers put

themselves on top of her enormous skirt, and they grew on there. But it looked so horrible that the painter, full of fright, decided to paint himself in the air in order to re-arrange them in the right order; for his brush was not long enough.

He did not paint himself plainly flat with a flat brush on flat canvas like the other painters who used to paint plain, flat figures – as you already know – on flat canvases, which were painted so flat that they really looked flat and plain, but he painted himself with his round brush round in the air. Then the wind came and blew him in the direction of the two figures. He kicked his legs in the air as much as he could, because he wanted to get to the place of the accident quickly, he slipped several times and fell, because still nobody had strewn ashes on the air.

Suddenly as he reached the two figures, he grew quite round in the middle, blew himself up, and burst not in two pieces, but in so many small parts that he could no longer be seen, and with him burst the ability of the painters to paint round figures round in the air with round brushes.

Therefore, painters now paint plain, flat figures with flat brushes on flat canvas.

THE IDIOT

There was once a fisherman who lived all alone upon an island with his wife. They were a God-fearing couple who had never harmed anyone in their lives, at least they appeared to be so. The seas were full of excellent fish and lobster and the fisherman and his wife were able to live contentedly and in comfort. On the shore of the mainland opposite was a small town in which lived a few fish merchants. They also were as innocent of all wrong as a well-trained house cat, at least to outward appearances.

One day the wife of the fisherman said to her husband: 'It will soon be time to mow the grass and make hay. We need some help. We also need someone to help with the fishing and take the fish to the town.'

'That is quite true', said the fisherman.

'Well, then, why not employ an idiot? Someone who is strong and willing to work, but hasn't got any brains. The government will give us money to feed him, but he won't know about that and we will be much better off than we are now.'

The fisherman agreed that this was a good scheme, so they looked about for an idiot. They soon found one and brought him to the island and set him to work.

But the wife wasn't satisfied. She said to her husband: 'We need money badly, everything is so expensive, and this is the season we are forbidden to catch lobster. It would be a good idea to catch some now. The tourists are coming, and soon the hotels will be full of them. They become angry if they cannot get lobster. Don't worry about the government regulations – no-one will mind because you will be doing good.'

'What about the idiot?' said the fisherman. 'He would tell?'

'He hasn't got the sense to know there is anything wrong.'

So the fisherman went out in the darkness with the idiot and they had a good catch. He was very happy thinking of the money he was going to make. He went to bed dreaming of lobsters and high prices.

But the idiot was also dreaming of lobsters and high prices. When the fisherman woke up he found the idiot, his boat and his lobsters were all gone.

The idiot went to the town, visited the first fish-merchant and said he had some lobster to sell. 'I'll take them of course', said the merchant, 'but don't tell anyone about it. You know that it is forbidden to catch lobster now.' The idiot promised, took the money, and now they went out together and the merchant watched him put the lobsters in his pot under cover of the morning mist.

But the idiot did not put the lobsters in the pot, though the merchant could not see this from the distance. Instead he went with the same lobsters to the second fish-merchant. He, like the first, was very glad to get the lobsters, gave the idiot the money for them and watched him put them into his own pot.

And so the idiot sold his lobsters in the same way to the third, the fourth and the fifth fish-merchant, until there were no more left in the town. Then he took them to the communal kitchen, sold them at a very low price and actually delivered them.

At lunch time the first merchant heard that the communal kitchen had lobster. Where did it come from? He went to his pot and found it empty. Then he went to the kitchen and said: 'Where did you get that lobster? It was stolen from my pot.' But they told him the idiot had sold it to them.

The second merchant was getting ready to sell the lobster to the big hotel, which needed it for the tourists, but he found his pot empty. He went out into the street, where he met the first merchant, and said to him: 'I bought some fish from the idiot, I saw him put it in my pot, and now it is empty.'

The first merchant answered: 'Now I know that your fish was not fish, but lobster, for I also bought some from the idiot, saw him put it in my pot, and now find it empty. Let's ask the other merchants if they have been tricked too.'

They all met and they decided that the idiot must be sent away. One of the merchants got out his boat and went over to the island and complained to the fisherman that the idiot had cheated him and that he, being his master, must pay for it.

The fisherman said he couldn't take responsibility, for the idiot had stolen the lobsters from him. The merchant realised, that there was nothing to be gained by accusing the fisherman further and said the idiot must be sent away.

In the meantime the idiot went to a public house and for the first time in his life went into the saloon bar. He drank so much that he was convinced it was the best day of his life. He thought so all the more when a small and very pleasant lady called Rosa came to help him drink, though he didn't notice that she took the rest of his money when he was drunk. But the barman did, and as the idiot's company was no longer wanted when he had no money left, he was thrown out.

Now he began to regret all the things he had done, and so he tried to lean on a wall and began to think of the future of his soul and all the good things that were in this world and the next, when along came a lady from the Salvation Army. She knew the idiot and she saw he was drunk.

'Do you regret what you have done?' she said, and as he regretted, she invited him to drink coffee and eat cake at the Salvation

Army hall. Soon he was singing piously, chanting hymns in praise of God, convinced that everything on earth is as it should be and that it would get steadily better and better, and still better.

When he had finished he took the boat and rowed back to the island, feeling quite depressed.

The fisherman was standing on the quay and the idiot was afraid that he would be severely punished. The fisherman told him to come inside, where he gave him coffee and cake, for he was a very good man, at least he appeared to be.

'I am not angry with you, my good fellow', he said. 'You have annoyed the fish merchants, who have annoyed me so many times before. Have some more coffee!'

THE LANDLADY

She was a lady! A lady? Much more!! A lady? Oh no! She was a Landlady!!

'I am not like other landladies', she used to say, 'you may speak to me, and when I say something, I say what I think. I say it to your face, not behind your back. Oh, Yes!! A landlady I am, and you may speak to me. For example, the government has ordered us to save fuel. When you use the gas, don't take a match, because that is fuel. Do it like me!! I take a piece of an old newspaper, the margin. You can read the paper without the margin; and take a light from the kitchen fire. I have time enough to spare, and you also have the time. If it is not successful and blows out on the way I try two or three times more. I am tough! Finally I get it to light the gas, and the match is saved. If you do that two or three times a day think how many matches you save in only one year. That is because I think! I am a thinking landlady!!!

Now you think it is done when you have saved the match. It is not. You can't save matches and waste gas. I don't mind whether it is your or my match, or whether you pay for the gas. Matches and gas are war weapons, and when the war is over they are peace weapons as well. How else could the government save matches? You see, I am a thinking landlady, and you may as well speak to me.

When you have lit the gas, I said 'You shall not waste gas'. Think twice before you start a job, and have the pot with water standing ready before you light the gas. Then you must not turn the gas too high and you must stand by until the water boils. The tea pot must stand ready with the tea leaves in. Don't put in too much tea or the tea will taste bitter. Immediately the water boils turn the gas out. That is easy and you save gas. I can see you from my place in the kitchen! Why else do you think I have mirrors on the wall: I can see into every room, and hear every noise in the whole house. For example, I sleep on the first floor, and when I go to bed I open my door. If I did not you might fall down the dark stairs and be killed without me hearing you. Yes! I am an intelligent landlady! You may speak to me.

As regards the staircase; I don't like you going up and downstairs. First take your boots off when you walk up my stairs, because boots ruin the carpet. I hear you also when you walk upstairs without boots.

You should not need to go up and downstairs more than two or three times in a day. It is up to your own will whether you go to the lavatory or the kitchen. Remember three times are allowed! Perhaps you go twice to the lavatory and once to the kitchen. I, for example, go only once a day to the lavatory. You may yourself easily get accustomed to that. And your room must be clean and tidy. It is strictly forbidden to use the room for working, cooking, or eating, only for sleeping from 10 p.m. to 7 a.m. The door has to be open and I make my visits unexpectedly, to see whether all is right. Don't use gas after five minutes past ten, and I don't like noises, for example whistling and singing. You are not a musician!

Yes I am a landlady! You may speak to me.

And now, will you pay the rent in advance?'

'My lady, My landlady! May I speak to you?'

'You may.'

'Would you allow me to look around for other accommodation?'

LONDON SYMPHONY

Halt, we are specialists.
To be let
To be sold
High class clothiers
Apply first floor
Artistic plumber
Enough said, we save you money.
Monarch hairdressing
Crime and Companion
A B C
Preston Preston Preston Preston
Bank
Bovril the power of beef
Bovril is good for you
John Pearce
Riverside 1698
What you want is Watney's
Dig for victory
Prize beers
Sell us your waste paper
Rags and Metals
Any rags any bones any bottles to-day
The same old question in the same old way
Milk bar
L M S
A B C
Tools of all kinds
All kinds of tools
Watney's Ales
Always something to eat
Monday to Friday
In a raid
Apply

A TRIBUTE TO KURT SCHWITTERS

E.L.T. Mesens

Not one week goes by but the art-gossip column of one or another French paper informs us that some known artist has acquired a Rolls-Royce, that another has been buying his fifth high-speed racing car, that a third is proprietor of two castles which used to belong to old aristocratic families, or that a fourth has added to his already well filled stables some remarkable and expensive race horse! And the artists concerned are not from the mundane-academical-portrait-painting set: they belong to the figurative or non-figurative *ultras*. Why not – the opportunist may say – while the going is good? Younger, lesser known painters and sculptors are paid in Paris, in New York and other centres, prices which *experimental* work never attracted before. Even in the reticent market of Britain, young and little known artists are nowadays paid twenty times higher prices than pre-war and *sell regularly* when equally talented colleagues could not attract the faintest attention for their work fifteen years ago and were doomed to near-starvation in the pre-war years! Evidently, capital investors, who do not care for meaning or quality, have found in the buying of works of art an excellent outlet for their overflowing money. On this fluorescently illuminated background, I cannot refrain from conjuring up a figure which remains in my memory in strong opposition to the present highlights of success: this figure of eternal childlike simplicity is that of the late Kurt Schwitters. He appears now as a far removed romantic personage, as if belonging to the Murger-Puccini exaggerated imagery and legend: the disinterested, careless, ever poor and idealistic exponent of something which had no material value or counterpart in the world in which he lived. However . . .

Kurt Schwitters' name was known to me in the very early twenties through reproductions of his work and texts appearing in many European *avant-garde* magazines – these publications were very numerous in those days of genuine *creation* and *dearth* of public understanding – and I admired his work almost at once. Schwitters' work had an immediate impact on me through its really revolutionary aspect, its unpretentious and completely anti-traditional effectiveness. I accepted Schwitters' poetry, collages and object-constructions with equally firm sympathy while I was at that time already critical of some exponents of late cubism and expressionism, and contemptuous of those artists whose work was already labelled *speculative merchandise*!

I still wonder why these *avant-garde* magazines were sent to me, as I was extremely young and hardly known outside of my immediate circle of friends. Still, I received these extraordinary publications as if, somewhere, a secret society knew which people would be caught in their spell. If there ever was such a 'secret society,' I express the wish not to have disappointed its members too much in the years which followed.

Since 1919, Schwitters was a regular contributor to 'Der Sturm' the review established in 1910, edited by Herwarth Walden in Berlin. This magazine managed to resist the rising Hitlerism until 1932 though losing little by little the quality and vigour of the numbers which appeared before 1914 – those crucial years when it stood, in Germany, for the young work of Chagall, Delaunay, Picasso, etc. . . . Schwitters remained wholeheartedly faithful to Walden which displeased, during the few years of the DADA-dictatorship in Germany (1918–1922), one of the originators of that movement in Zürich, Richard Hülsenbeck who became one of the principal leaders in Berlin. Hülsenbeck declared himself against all compromise with *decadent expressionists* and, in addition, demanded from his associates an open adherence to the revolutionary Marxism of that time. As far as *expressionism* was concerned, Schwitters had already far surpassed that: it was enough to look at his work to judge. But, as for a political attitude: all his life Schwitters adamantly refused to adopt one.

In spite of the ostracism of DADA-Berlin, from 1919 Schwitters was recognized by DADA-Zürich. He was therefore officially a *dadaist,* as he contributed two poems and two reproductions of constructions to the one and only number of 'Der Zeltweg'[1] and officially *merzist* because he was at the same time the founder and inventor of MERZ-activity.

Later, Schwitters contributed to several dadaist publications (except in France, where he was practically unknown), also post dadaist (such as the one number of 'Oesophage' published in Brussels in 1925, by René Magritte and myself) and *constructivist!* That the German constructivists had kept a weakness for MERZ-Schwitters is not too astonishing, because some of them were former Zürich-Dadas. I have never understood why other European constructivists had consideration for this militant *destructivist* whose message, all of sensibility, humour, and popular 'kitsch' combined, could win their approval even if not by extremely tortuous routes. The fashion at that time with the *constructivistes-hygénistes* was anti-sensibility and *formal logic* of the plastic work of art; *logic* about which the survivors have since had to lower their voices. I remember most clearly the anger which the quiet Piet Mondrian showed at the idea that his associate-theoretician Theo Van Doesburg could sink so low as to collaborate happily with Schwitters. Schwitters whom, he himself, Mondrian, took for an outcast of dadaism, and for disorder itself! (Even so, very much later, in New York, the same Mondrian expressed flattering opinions on the work of Max Ernst.)

In January, 1923, Schwitters started the publications of his own review named 'Merz' in Hanover. Between 1923 and 1932, he brought out twenty-four numbers, the last being entirely consecrated to his phonetic poem, the 'Ursonate' ('Primeval Sonata'). From time to time, I received certain numbers. Those which I have had good fortune to keep constitute captivating documents. They illuminate the path of the poet, artist, man of action, the detached individual who – in spite of collaborators of different horizons, often antinomic – lived quite isolated in his provincial town. In No.20, which served as catalogue for an exhibition (1927), Schwitters gives his reasons for MERZ-action. I quote them here without comment.

'In fact, I did not understand why one could not use in a picture, in the same way one uses colours made in a factory, materials such as: old tramway and bus tickets, washed up pieces of wood from the seashore, cloak-room numbers, bits of string, segments of bicycle wheels, in a few words, the whole bric-à-brac to be found lying about the lumber-room or on top of the dustbin. From my standpoint, it involved a social attitude, and, on the artistic level, a personal pleasure. What was important, I gave to my new manner of work, based on the use of these materials, the name of MERZ. This is the second syllable of the word KOMMERZ (commerce). This name was born out of one of my pictures: an image on which one reads the word MERZ, cut out of the KOMMERZ UND PRIVATBANK advertisement and stuck among abstract shapes. By some sort of unanimity of the other elements of the picture, this word became itself a part of the picture . . . And, when for the first time I exhibited these images made of paper, glue, nails, etc. . . . at the 'Der Sturm' Gallery in Berlin, I had to find a generic name to designate these new species. My work, indeed, did not answer to old classifications such as: Expressionism, Cubism, Futurism and all the others. Therefore I called all my pictures, considered as one kind, MERZ pictures, the name of the most characteristic one. Later, I extended this denomination, first

to my poetry – because I have written poems since 1917 – and finally to the whole of my corresponding activities. I, myself, am now called MERZ.'

One day, on finding a copy of the German art magazine 'Der Ararat' (No. 1 – second year – January, 1921), I was able to access the rapid pictorial and plastic-evolution achieved by Kurt Schwitters since his beginnings. In it there appeared an autobiographical article, entitled MERZ – as could be expected. The article was followed by two pages of poems and prose by the author. My slight knowledge of German just enabled me to detect in it some indications. Happily the whole was followed by seven very instructive reproductions, unfortunately not dated. The first reproduction represented a mourning woman – 'Die Trauernde' – near in style to the realistic work of the Münich School; the second – 'Stilleben mit Abendmahlskelch' – a still life technically very detailed, banal and in the academic style taught fifty years ago in art schools; the third – 'Hütten' – a cubist landscape showing the influence of Franz Marc. All of this evolution must have been effected between 1914, the year when the artist left the Dresden Academy, and 1918, when he exhibited for the first time his abstract oil paintings in Berlin. (I had to wait until 1956 to see certain of these works in the retrospective exhibition which circulated in Europe and was shown at the Palais des Beaux-Arts in Brussels). The four other reproductions in 'Der Ararat' were of a collage, two constructions and a sculpture-object dated 1920: in these four works Schwitters already spoke a completely personal language.

As Robert Motherwell remarked in the introduction of his Anthology:[2] *'The nature of Schwitters' work changed hardly at all up to the day of his death; it never lost its freshness, unpretentiousness, nor perfection of scale.'*

To these very pertinent affirmations of the American

painter-critic I shall only add some detail. Schwitters' constructions and collages of the German period were, in general, more *dramatic* in colour and accent than his work of the English period. As the artist at all times made use of the 'ready made' materials mainly, can we infer that those which he found in Hanover, in the course of his morning bicycle rides, were more *sombre* than those which he collected in the surroundings of Barnes or Ambleside? However it may be, he created in England a great number of collages very refined and often of an exquisite tenderness.

I only knew Schwitters personally about 1926–1927. I was in Paris, in a gallery on the left bank, one afternoon; Schwitters came in with Theo and Nelly Van Doesburg. Introductions were quickly made; there was no ice to break. A tall, solidly built man stood before me, like a baby on stilts naively smiling; the head of an artist, but with something of the rustic expression of the Hanoverian peasant. He asked the Van Doesburgs to invite me to a small reunion that same evening . . . It was to take place at the terrace of the Café des Deux Magots after dinner. I took with me the Belgian surrealist poet Camille Goemans. When we arrived, Schwitters, obviously in charge, presided over one or two tables round which we recognized Marcel Noll and, I think, Raymond Queneau, César Domela, Hans Arp, the Van Doesburgs and Tristan Tzara. From time to time, Schwitters recited by heart one of his poems or narrated one of his *Märchen*; each time heartily applauded by his small audience. Between each recitation we drank, so that a good number of saucers accumulated on the table near the honoured host. *'I have talked too much,'* he said at a certain moment, *'Here is the last poem.'* And he recited a piece in crescendo, at the end of which he seized a saucer and broke it on the edge of the table. Those who knew the poem already applauded; the rest of us were a bit dumb-founded, while several panic-stricken waiters dashed forward asking why a client should indulge in such acts. Tristan Tzara put his hand in his pocket and payed for the saucer, while Schwitters exclaimed: *'It is an Obligato! It is written in the text.'* And we all applauded and demanded an encore. The success was such that Schwitters had to repeat the same poem seven or eight times and, consequently, he broke seven or eight saucers. Tzara, well-known to the staff of the Deux Magots, paid the price of the saucer each time until one of the managers came to beg us to leave the establishment at once. The waiters were stupified that an individual voicing incomprehensible syllables punctuated at intervals by a saucer bursting into fragments received repeated enthusiastic applause. *And yet the broken porcelain was anticipated in the poem!* Schwitters was delighted with his evening. It was late. We separated.

The next day Goemans and I, had to return to Brussels and we decided to take a train in the evening. Arriving at Gare du Nord, who did we find on the platform? Schwitters, accompanied to his train by the Van Doesburgs! He had a 3rd class return ticket to Hanover and the compartments of this class were full to overflowing. We were travelling 2nd. We had to find a compromise. We offered to pay Schwitters' supplement as far as Brussels. This he refused with the utmost energy. We got into a 2nd class carriage where there was room and next to a 3rd class carriage. Schwitters got into the 3rd class carriage where even the corridors were full of people and luggage. So that he could talk to us, he installed himself, balanced on the two metal plates which serve as gangway from one coach to another. The noise of the train was such that our conversation could only be carried on in shouts composed of German, Platt-Deutsch and French words. Each time a conductor passed and disturbed our trio, Schwitters retreated to the 3rd class side as though scared at the idea of having to pay a supplement. He confessed to us later that he had not much money left in his pocket. At our repeated offer to pay the 2nd class surcharge for him and to lend him a little pocket money he categorically refused a second time, saying that he disliked to borrow money and particularly from people younger than he. Schwitters wore a thick flannel shirt and a celluloid collar. His only luggage was a very small suitcase. When the Belgium customs officers passed, he had to open his case in which there was only a change of celluloid collar and a bundle of Merz publications. He held out the collar to one of the customs' men and said to him in German with a smile: *'This is inflammable!'* and, indicating his books, he added, *'These also perhaps.'* The customs officer who had obviously understood nothing, shrugged his shoulders and went off. As we arrived at Bruxelles-Midi our shouted conversation ended. Schwitters had to change trains at Bruxelles-Nord. We took leave of him with regret. We were all three covered with smuts!

Schwitters' travels are famous. Mies van der Rohe tells one[3] and Hannah Höch tells another in great detail,[4] which surpasses by far the one I just related.

When I arrived in England, in 1936, not many people knew about Schwitters, except a few Mid-European refugees among whom were some former professors of the Bauhaus-Dessau. I am pretty sure that the first work of Schwitters was added to an English collection as late as 1937. It is a beautiful small collage dated 1920, originating from the French poet Eluard's early harvests, which then became part of the Penrose Collection.

But it was in 1938 that the exhibition of 'Modern German Art' took place in London.[5] The art which was designated by the Nazis as 'degenerate.' It included some works of Schwitters. Here I must not let slip the chance to rectify, at last, an error which has been endlessly repeated for ten years in notices appearing, outside of England, on Schwitters. After the death of the artist there appeared a notice, in a Swiss weekly, I believe, very well intentioned indeed, in which it said that works by Schwitters had been shown *'in the exhibition of Degenerate Art at the Tate Gallery in London.'* The very competent and careful bio-bibliographer Hans Bolliger repeated this error in his 'Résumé chronologique de la vie de l'oeuvre de K.S.'[6] Since, this résumé has been reprinted without any correction, in the catalogue K.S. (No. 152, June, 1956) of the Stedelijk Museum in Amsterdam and in that of the Palais des Beaux Arts in Brussels (October–November, 1956). But in fact, in 1938 Great Britain was not at war with Germany. How could the Tate Gallery, a state-controlled institution, organize an exhibition described as 'manifestation against the exhibitions 'Entartete Kunst'?' The diplomatic aspect of such a gesture would have been in direct contradiction with the famous umbrella journey of Prime Minister Chamberlain! No, the exhibition of 'Modern German Art' took place at the 'New Burlington Galleries' – organized by a private committee (of clearly anti-Nazi tendencies) and had for patrons half a dozen names of world celebrity.

We know that Schwitters left Germany for Norway in 1935; that, after the invasion of that country in 1940, he took refuge in England and that he had to pass several months in an internment camp.

The painter Fred Uhlman, who was in the same camp, has often told me about this period so depressing for most of those interned. But Schwitters' biographers have not yet told us that our friend was as happy as a lark there. No material worries, regular meals, rest at normal hours and, *nearly every evening* re-unions of intellectuals exchanging views on art and philosophical matters. There Kurt shone in all his glory. At any time his audience could always count on him: he told his stories each day more and more enriched with detail and recited his poems endlessly . . . The *Ursonate* must have been recited from beginning to end numbers of times.

The simplicity, the unfailing good nature of Schwitters won

for him the special esteem of the camp commandant. The latter occasionally had one of the guardians fetch Schwitters to his home to allow him to work freely on collages or to make sketches. Perhaps Schwitters had proposed to make his portrait . . . ? For it must not be forgotten that, throughout the span of his life as artist, from Hanover to Ambleside, Schwitters had to paint portraits to earn his living! Portraits in a style sufficiently mild not to displease a provincial and bourgeois clientèle.

During the war, Schwitters paid me two or three visits at Hampstead. At that period R.A. Penrose purchased another collage from him and I bought two small works. Perhaps some of his refugee friends also bought something from him at some time? In 1944 the picturesque Jack Bilbo organized a Schwitters exhibition in his 'Modern Art Gallery.' I doubt if this was either a moral or selling success.

When the war was over, I visited Schwitters who occupied a house in Barnes. Though not rich, he looked quite happy. A very devoted young woman was taking care of him. In view of the re-opening of the 'London Gallery' in new premises, I bought a certain number of works from him. When he was later living at Ambleside, the 'London Gallery' organized two MERZ Poetry Recitals. Their reception by the public was characteristic of the post-war mind. If I say that there was a total lack of interest, I am not exaggerating! At the first reading, on Wednesday, 5th March, 1947, the attendance was of sixteen people including two journalists; at the second reading, on Friday 7th March, there were twelve people! Schwitters recited with all his magic and afterwards he was charming, never allowing himself to be discouraged . . . But his heart was already in a bad state. He died ten months later.

In April-May, 1950, towards the end of the London Gallery's existence, I organized 'An Homage to Kurt Schwitters' bringing together thirty-three exhibits and some documentation on the artist. At the private view, a director of our company, the late Peter Watson, said to me: '*They are quite nice, these things. But it's DADA, it's twenty years too late, my dear*!' I curtly answered: '*Not twenty . . . it's thirty years too late.*' For public (and collectors alike) it was TEN YEARS TOO EARLY.

At present in London, the 'Lord's Gallery' invites us to see one hundred and thirteen works by Kurt Schwittwers. At the same time two works are shown with the Urvater Collection, presented by the Arts Council, in turn in Leicester, in York, and later at the Tate Gallery. In the Brussels World Fair's '50 years of Modern Art,' three remarkable Schwitters are shown neighbouring subtle and supreme Klees. In Düsseldorf, at the DADA retrospective, thirty-five of his works are hung and in New York, two appear on the catalogue of Sidney Janis's '10th Anniversary Exhibition.' All that, and perhaps more elsewhere, is on view NOW. All this excitement round his work, now!

Poor Schwitters, if he were alive, he would think it a dream! And it isn't.

1 'Der Zeltweg', Editors: Otto Flake, Dr Walter Serner and Tristan Tzara. Published by Verlag Mouvement Dada, Zürich, Novemeber 1919.
2 'The Dada Painters and Poets'. Edited by Robert Motherwell, Wittenborn, Schultz, Inc., New York, 1951.
3 'The Dada Painters and Poets', (Introduction, page xxi).
4 'DADA – Dokumente einer Bewegung' catalogue for exhibition at Kunstverein für die Rheinlande und Westfalen, Düsseldorf Kunsthalle, 5 September – 19 October 1958, and later in Frankfurt and Amsterdam.
5 'Modern German Art' by Peter Thoene – a Pelican Special (S6) first published by Penguin Books, Ltd., in 1938.
6 'Kurt Schwitters, collages' – page 24 – the lovely little catalogue published by Berggruen et Cie, Paris, 1953.

This article was first published in *Art News and Review*, Sat. 11 Oct. 1958, vol.x, no.19, pp.5–7.

LETTER FROM ERNST SCHWITTERS TO *ART NEWS AND REVIEW*

Dear Sir,
I was very pleased to read E.L.T Mesens' long and warm 'Tribute to Kurt Schwitters', in connection with the present exhibition at Lord's Gallery. As Mr. Mesens himself points out in his article, errors tend to be repeated endlessly unless checked. As son of Kurt Schwitters, and his close collaborator for more than 25 years, I feel it my duty to correct some important errors of the 'Tribute' at the outset.

One is the last sentence of the Tribute: 'Poor Schwitters, if he were alive, he would think it a dream!' By 'it', of course, is meant the recognition of Kurt Schwitters as one of the most important pioneers of Modern Art during the ten years after his death in 1948. In fact Kurt Schwittters most certainly would not have considered it 'a dream' at all! True, he was a remarkably modest person, but he was too, at all times, even during the worst intellectual and personal persecutions, entirely sure of himself and his art, and of the importance he would have on the development of art. He never faltered once in this connection.

In his article 'I and my goals' in No. 21 of the MERZ- magazine with the subtitle 'Veilchen' (Violets) Kurt Schwitters, explaining among other things his famous 'MERZ-Bau' in Hanover, goes on to say: 'The MERZ-Bau is a typical Violet, which blossoms in hidden places, but I am not. I know that I am important as a factor in the development of Art, and always will remain so. I say this with all possible emphasis, so that nobody afterwards can say: "The poor old man didn't even know, how important he was". No, I am not stupid, nor am I shy. I know for sure that the Great Time will come for me and all other important personalities of the abstract movement, when we will influence an entire generation. . . . What we are expressing in our works is neither idiocy nor subjective play, but the expression of our time itself.'

Regarding Kurt Schwitters' internment in this country after his arrival on June 16th 1940 as a refugee from Nazi-occupied Norway, he was interned for 17 months and he was not 'as happy as a lark there'. In fact he was so downhearted that a very old epileptic ailment which had disappeared with adolescence, recurred, and he had several cruel fits. For the outward world he always tried to put up a brave show, but in the quietness of the room I shared with him during the few months we were allowed together in internment, his painful disillusion was clearly revealed to me. I was released 4 months before my father, and his letters from internment are sad documents of this final and so unnecessary humiliation. Kurt Schwitters worked with more concentration than ever during internment to stave off bitterness and hopelessness, and he was not 'occasionally fetched by guards to the home of the camp-commander to paint there', but he was allotted an attic in the administration building of the camp, outside the barbed wires, where he worked regularly every day.

Kurt Schwitters did not 'leave Germany for Norway in 1935', but in January 1937. However he visited Norway every year between 1929 and 1937. When Nazi-tyranny became absolutely unbearable, he decided to stay in Norway, never to return to Germany. My father's books had been burned at the infamous Auto-da-fé of 1934. Shortly afterwards his works were removed from all German Public Galleries and Museums and pilloried at the 'Entartete Kunst' (degenerate art) Exhibition.

A widely repeated misconception is that Kurt Schwitters 'had to paint portraits in order to make a living'. True, he did paint portraits, and, even more, landscapes in an impressionistic style. He did sell these more easily that his pioneering work, and that helped him over the worst times. However he did not paint naturalistically solely to make a living; on the contrary it was his often expressed conviction that the human mind eventually becomes stale if it does not receive new impressions constantly through the study of nature. And certainly this study of nature is everywhere apparent in the abstract work of Kurt Schwitters which is never formal, cold and logical, but always shows the warmth and richness of tone-values of nature, and also always makes use of objects found in nature.

Lastly Mr. Mesens relates Piet Mondrian's anger about the close collaboration between Kurt Schwitters and Theo Van Doesburg. In fact Piet Mondrian collaborated with my father quite closely in several numbers of the MERZ-magazine with reproductions of his work as well as with articles about his aims.

Yours faithfully
Ernst Schwitters

REPLY FROM E.L.T. MESENS IN *ART NEWS AND REVIEW*

To the Editor,
Dear Sir,
Mr. Ernst Schwitters tells us that he was his father's 'close collaborator for more than 25 years'. For most of Kurt Schwitters' old friends and admirers this is a revelation. On the strength of this 'close collaboration' he goes on to correct 'some important errors' in my Tribute. But WHY DID Mr. Ernst Schwitters NEVER TAKE THE TROUBLE TO CORRECT THESE ERRORS BEFORE?

More than a year before K.S. died, Carola Giedion-Welcker published her «Anthologie der Abseitigen» (Berne, 1946) and the same author wrote a very enthusiastic article on our friend in the Swiss paper 'Die Weltwoche' dated 15 August 1947. In both, biographical note in the book and study in the weekly paper, Mrs. Giedion gives the wrong date of K.S. departure to Norway without being corrected by the artist. Since the death of K.S. the 'wrong' date and other errors have been repeated again and again. Particularly, Hans Bolliger's «Résumé chronologique», which has been reprinted several times in catalogues of exhibitions of which Mr. Ernst Schwitters was co-organiser!

Mr. Ernst Schwitters takes the opportunity to mix questions of data with personal and artistic appreciation. For those of us who knew and liked K.S., the ways in which we picture his personality and the ways in which we so highly appreciate his work, are matters which cannot be ensured by his son.

I do not wish to enter here into the later part of the history of the «De Stÿl» group, which would be necessary in order to answer Mr. Ernst Schwitters' innocent statement referring to Piet Mondrian. I knew most of the members of «De Stÿl» closely enough. But the petty-history is not relevant enough to the case of K.S. I simply state here that Mondrian never 'contributed' to MERZ, even if reproductions of his work and text were printed in this magazine.

Yours sincerely,
E.L.T Mesens

Ernst Schwitter's letter (p.29) appeared in *Art News and Review*, Sat. 25 Oct. 1958, vol.x, no.20, p.8.
E.L.T. Mesens' reply appeared in *Art News and Review*, Sat. 8 Nov 1958, vol.x, no.21, p.11.